# MARC BROWN

# ARTHUR'S FIRST KISS

## Step into Reading® Sticker Books

### Random House 🏠 New York

Copyright © 2001 by Marc Brown. All rights reserved under International and Pan-American Copyright Conventions. Published in the United States by Random House, Inc., New York, and simultaneously in Canada by Random House of Canada Limited, Toronto.

www.randomhouse.com/kids

*Library of Congress Cataloging-in-Publication Data*
Brown, Marc Tolon. Arthur's first kiss / Marc Brown. p. cm. (Step into reading)
SUMMARY: Even though she has not been invited to the party,
D.W. manages to save Arthur from having to kiss Francine.
ISBN 0-375-80602-4 (trade) — ISBN 0-375-90602-9 (lib. bdg.)
[1. Aardvarks—Fiction. 2. Animals—Fiction. 3. Parties—Fiction. 4. Kissing—Fiction.
5. Brothers and sisters—Fiction.] I. Title. II. Step into reading.
PZ7.B81618Apmk 2001 [E]—dc21 00-038714
Printed in the United States of America January 2001 10 9 8 7 6 5 4 3 2 1

STEP INTO READING, RANDOM HOUSE, and the Random House colophon are registered trademarks
and the Step into Reading colophon is a trademark of Random House, Inc.
ARTHUR is a registered trademark of Marc Brown.

School was out for the weekend.
"See you at my party tomorrow,"
Francine said to Arthur and Buster.

"Don't forget. It's at my house," said Muffy.

The two girls ran off,
whispering and giggling.
"So are you REALLY going to kiss
Francine tomorrow?"
Buster asked Arthur.
"What!" yelled Arthur.
"Well, that's what Francine
is telling everyone," said Buster.

"No!" said Arthur.

"I'd rather kiss a frog."

The next day, Arthur got dressed
for the party.
He wore his new yellow sweater
and a red bow tie.

"Oh, you are so handsome,
lover boy," laughed D.W.
Arthur turned as red as a beet.

"I want to go to the party, too,"
said D.W.

"No!" said Arthur.

"I'll be your bodyguard,"
she said. "I'll keep Francine
from kissing you."

"If you really want to help," said Arthur, "you can take Pal for a walk later."

Arthur walked to Muffy's house
and rang the bell.
"I hope they don't play
that bottle kissing game,"
he said to himself.

The party was
in the family room.
There were balloons and party hats
and a table with lots of food.

All of Arthur's friends were there.
"Relax," Buster said to Arthur.
"Francine said we won't play
spin-the-bottle."

Francine and Muffy were busy
doing something in the corner.

"I'm writing each boy's name

on a piece of paper for a game,"

Francine said to everyone.

But she didn't write

each boy's name.

She wrote only Arthur's name.

Then she folded the pieces of paper

and put them in a hat.

And Muffy said, "I'm writing

the girls' names."

But she wrote only Francine's name.

"The boy who picks his own name
will be kissed by the girl
who picks her own name!"
said Muffy.
The boys all groaned.

"Here, Arthur, you try first," said Muffy.

"I don't want to play," said Arthur.

"Oh, come on," said Buster. "Take a chance."

Arthur picked a piece of paper.
It said "Arthur."
"Oh, no!" he moaned.

Outside, D.W. was walking Pal.

"Muffy lives here," she said.

"Let's do a little party snooping."

D.W. peeked into the window.

She saw Muffy tie a scarf

around Arthur's eyes.

Then Muffy led him to the garage.

"Oh, oh," said D.W.

"The kissing game."

D.W. put her ear

next to the window.

She heard Muffy say,

"Now it's the girls' turn.

You go first, Francine."

"Come on, Pal," said D.W.

"Only YOU can save Arthur now."

D.W. ran to the garage.

The door had a tiny flap

for Muffy's cat to go in and out.

D.W. opened the flap

and pushed Pal through it.

Pal was happy to see Arthur.

He jumped on the workbench

and gave Arthur a great big kiss.

Then another and another.

"Stop it, Francine!" said Arthur.

Francine came into the garage
just as Arthur ripped off the scarf.
"It's kissy-kissy time," she said.
"Run for your life!" yelled D.W.
And Arthur did.

Arthur brought a piece of cake
home for D.W.

"Thanks, D.W.," he said.

"You're a great bodyguard."

And he had something

for Pal, too—

a great big kiss.